A deserted woman
her husband lusts t
widower retraces the last European holiday he took with his wife. Excursions are made into the personal and political absurdities of language and naming. Whether it's a bus tour in Mumbai, a café stop in Lausanne, or a sunset walk along the Bay of Bengal – Ven Begamudré's journeys are filled with longing, desire and a tenderness that persists beyond reason. This is *The Lightness Which Is Our World, Seen from Afar*.

Also by Ven Begamudré:

Short Stories
Laterna Magika
A Planet of Eccentrics

Novels
The Phantom Queen
Sacrifices
Van de Graaff Days

Biography
Isaac Brock: Larger than Life

The Lightness Which Is Our World, Seen from Afar

Ven Begamudré

We are at home with one another,
we are each other's home,
the voice in the doorway
calling *Come in, come in,*
it's growing dark.

Lorna Crozier, from "Living Day by Day"

for Dr. Inayat Shah
some magical + sometimes
humourous, sometimes
sad poetry
with all best wishes
from Ven Begamudré
Regina, Jan. 2011

Frontenac House
Calgary, Alberta

Copyright © 2006 by Ven Begamudré

All rights reserved, including moral rights. No part of this publication may be reproduced or transmitted in any form or by any means electronic or mechanical including photocopying, recording, or any information storage retrieval system without permission in writing from the author or publisher, or ACCESS copyright, except by a reviewer or academic who may quote brief passages in a review or critical study.

Book and cover design: Epix Design
Cover art: Shelley Sopher
Author photo: Lynne Beclu
Excerpt from "Living Day By Day" from *Inventing the Hawk* by Lorna Crozier. Used by permission of McClelland & Stewart Ltd.

Library and Archives Canada Cataloguing in Publication

Begamudré, Ven, 1956-
The lightness which is our world, seen from afar / Ven Begamudré.

Poems.
ISBN 1-897181-02-7

Title.

PS8553.E342L44 2006 C811'.54 C2005-907653-4

We acknowledge the support of the Canada Council for the Arts which last year invested $20.3 million in writing and publishing throughout Canada. We also acknowledge the support of The Alberta Foundation for the Arts.

Printed and bound in Canada
Published by Frontenac House Ltd.
1138 Frontenac Avenue S.W. Calgary, Alberta, T2T 1B6, Canada
Tel: 403-245-2491 Fax: 403-245-2380
editor@frontenachouse.com www.frontenachouse.com

1 2 3 4 5 6 7 8 9 10 09 08 07 06

For Daniel and Wendy Coleman.

This book is also for Patrick Lane, who lit my way without realizing that he carried a lamp; for Jay Meek, who, without meaning to, reminded me that there are still gentlemen in this world; and for Lorna Crozier, who told me long ago, one summer at Fort San, "Oh, Ven, your poetry is so awful, you should stick to writing fiction."

Contents

The Lightness Which Is Our World, Seen from Afar

One: Beligge, Pakshigalu, Prema

1: Ondu

She remembers how he railed
as a householder. His obsession
with rain, his need for it
to purge their previous life, promise
an end to rebirth. In the compound
are ninety-nine images he crafted of summer:
unglazed, even unfired,
pieces of some greater whole that holds
his longing for what summer could have been.
She dreams he will return in her lifetime
to finish them.

2: Eradu

There is a glimmer of dew; still every mouth is dry. He watches
parakeets circling without rest. Hopes if he must be reborn,
he will return as a partridge fed on moonbeams. Cobras stifle
in the dust. If he had a child he would not want it to hear
parakeets without songs.

3: Muru

Vultures alight on the banyans.
They are heavy with flesh.

There is no rain
in a land where crocodiles weep.

This is what she hates. So much thirst
and how blue the sky.

4: Nalku

Even as a woman denying her loneliness
thinks of summer as a season for desertion,
thus couplets are composed of unlikely lines
and so much sadness emerges: the princess
hoping for a true prince who will not scorn her
for her flaws or learning or wit. He is merely
a dream, this long-lost mate, as if
the thought *We remember* is all she needs
to recapture their previous life. It is
never enough. She knows this.

5: Aidu

Shadows lengthen by a stroke, his need not hers. He thinks of the Adivasi, those original tribes. How the girls sleep together, unripe yet welcoming nightly visits of boys. The boy pretending to abduct the girl. The dowry to appease her clan. How simple their desires: shamans interpreting intentions of everyday gods; no need for clothing, coyness, shame; bands of cloth barely meeting in the back. He sighs, holding himself tight, a lone cloud refusing to weep.

6: Aru

Pausing near an evergreen banyan,
she eyes tourists at the temple
well after nightfall performing *pujas*
at the end of a picnic. All these prayers
for the boredom to end. She likes
to watch the Brahmins, their circling
disk of flame, the neon lights.
What she likes best is to hover
when worshippers leave the sanctum
for the muddle in the courtyard;
how they reclaim sandals
they know by feel, *ayahs*
shepherding children, parents
frowning at a hand-cranked carousel
creaking through the night. She listens
while novices close the inner gates
to guard the sleeping god. Inside
the Brahmins fatten on sugar and *ghee,*
making the best of this age
before the white horse comes,
Kalki with his sword blazing
like the comet of doom.

7: Elu

Hunger yet nothing will grow except doubt and envy. Where do all the songs go? What he craves is flight, an end to gravity, everyone becoming lighter. Hunger much as the Adivasi know scrabbling for roots while that other hunger wanes, the hunger for flesh. All their doubts like *Why?* and *How?* In this case, the phrase *much as* easing his pangs. Hunger and doubt and envy, the day growing hot.

8: Entu

She is chanting the end of *Ramayana,*
not the first end, not the one children
are told: when Rama takes Sita back
home, the long road north lit by lamps.
It is the second end she likes: when Sita
stands accused of seducing her abductor.

It is a tale for autumn nights
told in the breeze: the endless
quest for that perfect love.

How comforting it would be,
she thinks, if there were only one end:
no question of Rama's faith
or questioning of Sita; no need for tears
from listeners or lovers. Yet the version
she prefers, her *Ut-Ramayana,*
is so much more like life.

9: Ombaththu

He reaches out and touches scales. Each night the cobra seems more tame. He ponders the skin shrinking and splitting, shedding and drying with such ease. Beneath the slackened hood, an emerald. He will harvest it without killing his lone visitor, condemning himself to death from its mates. First the bites, then his fleeting breath. Their justice too swift, his execution slow. He could never do it, he thinks. He plucks a scale from the hood, sucks at the root where it is moist, the blood green, and savours it. Is this how she saw him, resenting her need? He urges the cobra towards him. He thinks, *When it leaves to rejoin its kind, I will warn it of the sun.*

10: Haththu

Her *Ut-Ramayana* is ambiguous.
The first end led naturally to rain.
Not the warm rains of winter here.
A rain that plunges in relief
on summer afternoons,
a rain that leaves its mark.
The second end, as perverse as life,
leads instead to grief. She
recites the paradox to herself,
envying the poet his foresight:

The presence of doubt
is the nature of love.

Often she wishes Rama failed in his rescue;
let Sita save herself. Yet *Ramaraj*
could not have begun, the perfect reign
of an imperfect king, that once or ever.

11: Hannondu

Allow me to intrude. This is not some local diversion, didactic entertainment with an easy plot. We are what the Goddess dreams, able to direct her inventions as easily as we command the sun. Consider the footprints on a river bank after the Goddess crosses the river. We call it a sign but it is only she, walking in her sleep. Another way of being, which we envy. The question to be answered: *Yet why are we here?* The Goddess chuckling in her sleep when we seem so real.

Two: Hagalu, Nagarahavu, Kopa

12: Hanneradu

The beggars have discovered her home.
A legless man propels himself at ease
on a wheeled board followed by a woman
cursing God for their lack of sons,
though she has no tongue. A girl without ears
dangles earrings on either side of her face;
swears she would never disfigure the child in her,
not above the neck. Every well is dry.
The icebox, as elsewhere, is locked.

Their hostess is in a dark room
clutching a statue: a goddess of erotic love.
She must emerge to greet the intruders
and feed them but for once she is not angry
with this image of summer, unfinished
like so much he began. She tells herself
he was not to blame and cups the breasts.
They are glazed and firm.

13: Hadimuru

He lies with his face to the old moon and tunes his ears to their whispering, the hooded hiss of the guardians. He will creep with them to the edge of their realm. He prays the night will not be too dark. He prays the many portals will be lit by the brilliance hoarded within. Inside he will discard his loincloth, shed his fears. Squirm his way down through their halls: here, in the labyrinths they rule. And yet he will not touch the stones. He will keep only the thrill of resisting temptation, prizing this above the emeralds, rubies and diamonds of night.

14: Hadinalku

All of us hunger alone. Beggars
wander, letting no one hold them back
with promises. No water to be had,
yet so much time for thirst.

The goddesses of dawn and dusk
are sisters. She mouths this and reaches
down in her shadows, aching to be full.
She feels nothing at her fingertips
but heat, resenting her need,
his restlessness, while beggars cackle
and a wheeled board creaks, the passing
shapes a reminder of life beyond the shades.

15: Hadinaidu

Cobras in these thick summer months shrivel within their loosening skins. Shrivel and coil themselves on the hoard that galls them, drives them from cool halls into a sun blinding them to their duty. The cobras, the hooded ones.

16: Hadinaru

Dancing in her still dark room
she welcomes a four-armed god:
he so dazzling she closes her eyes
to his touch; she so ready she mounts him
before he warns her of the outcome,
ruining her for mere men.

17: Hadinelu

The man creeps again to their haunts. Trailing his loincloth,
he enters to squeeze himself through mazes to this: a ransom
left for his taking, light into light. He tells himself to relish his
conquest. Soon. If there is any vestige approaching lust it is for
these gems knotted in the cloth. He crawls back to the hut, his
skin rasping through dust like scales.

18: Hadinentu

Her cries fade, ebbing like the light
from her impossible lover's face.

If she lies perfectly still in his arms
she can hear a keening while the hooded ones writhe.

19: Haththombaththu

Let us be frank: for the man to creep at night in search of
wealth is just another error in judgement, as a lion makes who
leaves cover to be confronted by his trackers. To surrender to
the surprise of life: now this is stoicism, the kind we Hindus
are thought to have perfected. Even you cannot hope to resist
it. *Satyagraha*. Soul force. No surprise the Mahatma lives. No
surprise you still mistake what he did for the passiveness of
a sea on calm days while under the surface waters churn: the
peace of doves the one thing a sea cannot attain, as dust cannot
know it is even in the eyes of a lion a cause for tears.

Three: Rathri, Ane, Shoka

20: Ippaththu

She lies with her god on a mat, starlight
piercing the shutters to dapple his arms,
two cradling her, two crossed upon his breast
rising and falling with his breath. The god dreams
creation, the cries of children in the sun,
food their only thought. And shade.
The image she tries to forget is of a man
moulding a child out of clay.

The arms release her when she rises
to open the shutters. She says, *Love
is for dreamers.* This is what the god read
in thoughts she could not speak:
children in a monsoon playing with toys,
the rain sweeping away the stars
and the rootless seeds.

21: Ippathondu

What the god finds on earth is what Manu forgot in the flood: the tracks he left filling into themselves, generations to come chafing at rebirth. The full load, the seeds rooted once more, *pujas* that are prayers of *Why?* The god cares nothing for this. He has come down in lust and learned sorrow. The footprints on the river bank are not even his. How touching his surprise, his arms thrashing in the heat. A wonderful irony: his consort waiting and he knowing he has been found out. If he were a man he could say, *She meant nothing to me.*

22: Ippaththeradu

Then there is the man who does not want to die rich. When it finally rains he will leave with nothing more than the clothes on his pilgrim back. This is how he wants to be remembered. This is the tale they will tell when the sun no longer raves. He is planning to head farther south. He will leave only if everything else survives this drought in which even the young have no will.

23: Ippaththamuru

Clouds appear with a rising sun,
lacy black in the dawn: the grieving clouds.

How many lives. How many ages.
Vultures wake to circle the compound.

24: Ippaththanalku

There is little strength to breathe left in the elephant plodding through the mud. It is as grey as the rain. If you could read the embroidered script on its cap you might see *Come to the Circus*, an invitation the man fears. The chance to laugh without guilt. He longs for it the way he longs for all those old verses by Tagore, rivers teeming with golden fish, prayers for the ease of innocent days.

25: Ippaththaidu

She sees the elephant looming through rain
breaking figures in the compound. Lumbering
from bench to kiln while pondering the number
ninety-nine as though their maker must repent.
This is wishful thinking: an animal
hoping for completion with only memory
to goad it. No wonder she pictures vultures
rising from the banyans, laughing, expecting
only fragments to greet their return.

26: Ippaththaru

Darkness surrounds him in his hut. He lies with his limbs exposed to the hooded ones. They take back the gems he holds, slithering across his thighs, hissing at each other, then at the lone visitor who glides away and coils into itself well beyond their reach. This is how Manu must have felt on the mountain, he thinks, water everywhere beneath his boat, the bitterness of triumph, clutching the many seeds he saved, returning them to soil and silt and stones. These last the preserve of the guardians.

27: Ippaththelu

The flesh left on branches is a horror
she ignores while she gathers the fragments
and cradles them. Rain plucks the trees clean.
How she yearns for night, the four-armed god
returning with his emerald coloured seed
and still it sprouts and withers and dies.
She is not ready, she thinks, to bear a child
for a god, one so dazzling she cannot face him
when he enters. Yet even riding him she thinks
of a man with two hands moulding a child
to which he gives his mouth, her eyes. This
is what poisoned their love: thirst because someone
has to light their pyre. Hunger because nothing will do
except their own flesh and blood.

28: Ippaththentu

It is a vestige of the rains he absently moulds: wet clay malleable as an infant learning to sing. He could change it into anything he wants. He could even make a child in his own image, bring it to life with fire. He cradles the form in the sun on his hands, hardening while the moisture returns to the earth and air. He tells himself some things were never meant to be. Not in this life, perhaps not ever.

Itineraries

1: The Sound, the Scents of an Evening Air

At the outdoor tables of the Hotel D'Angleterre
below Cité de Cathédrale,
I marvel how the smell of perfume
has been swirling about us today,
even on our ferry on Lac Léman
when, this morning, leaving Vevey,
we saw strollers who turned back
and forth at the chains – anchored there.
Then, as we neared our destination
within sight of the carousel,
we saw a mime on the lip of a fountain
with a parasol balanced on her palm.
How vulnerable we become in crossing,
having to choose our vantage
between what we're leaving and what we're
approaching with little to guide us,
no more able to ask advice of strangers
than the driver of one taxi
seemed willing to. For you
I glean pleasure in embarking, disembarking,
while we criss-cross a long curved lake
randomly choosing times of departure
according to the arc of the swell.
Yet we were never taken unaware:
it was the fathomless lake we loved,
the resorts waking to life each day,
and we envied those who could linger
for the promise of a warming sun
with overcoats and scarves they bore,
took off, shrugged on again.

There was one girl, climbing steps,
who stumbled though her father held her
when he called to his wife, "*Attends!*"

This evening as I think of their girl
a golden retriever noses under tables
where the perfumed ladies dine,
so that even as you order *café noir*
I smell something damp and pink
rising from the roses and peonies,
still fragrant since our arrival
at Lausanne, where we've missed our plane.

2: Kanton Bern

Staying around the corner from two minor embassies,
I walk up Junkergasse to the Plattform
where mornings I read –
one of the early risers who relish the frost.

From where I sit I can look up at the Münster,
the knobbly spire foreshortened,
its tracery less severe at night.
Here Berchtold the Fifth hunted *bären*, bears,

and this morning in the bustle displacing
the peace of doves, I become aware
the Swiss keep dogs
the way they keep time – moving, mechanical, leashed.
I'm baffled by myself.

Only last Sunday, in Lausanne on the Quai D'Ouchy
where Byron himself stayed
at the Hotel D'Angleterre and casually wrote
The Prisoner of Chillon,

I felt so envious of his death, those lines.
How much we owe, beyond reckoning.
I look up at the idols tumbling about me,

sheltered in a park of slumbering chestnuts,
furious at my loss of power.
Sometimes with no cause I have been arrogant
in the presence of strangers,

and often denied the aristocrat
others could see in me, unreasonable
at the wrong wicket for reservations
or at a museum,
calling it a poor apology for war.

The frost is gone. Grandfathers arrive to play chess,
passing students move the heavy stone pieces.
Below, along the Aare, birds ignore pylons:
mallards, trumpeter swans
all swim with their young as though in the wild.

There must be a simple way to carry baggage.
Relaxed, graceful, forgiving,
I wish I could learn what to do with my fury.

3: Walking the Old Town

Evenings, crusty dragons amble from their caves
to sigh in the cobbled plaza
while a white oak, erect, guards its opinions,
knowing age is hobbling old friends
with braces and stays,
no longer aroused by virgins or knights-errant.
We lie exposed to weak beams
snagging on the cathedral, sunlight that refracts
in the oak leaves
and surrounds branches like illumined incense,
transforming the plaza
into some exotic venue
without complicated invocations of magic.

I have no prayers for myself, no salvation planned.
I want your life to be spared, blessed.
I want you to keep walking as far as we vowed,
the beams flowing
past the rose window of the cathedral
while you lift your voice,

unashamed of its wistfulness,
unashamed of all we have made or unmade.

4: Comune di Siena

Sunday, the Palazzo Ravizza might have been a museum
whose empty garden could hold no sound,
and in the square called the Field, Il Campo,
a guest waiter in a waistcoat folded his gloved hands
and looked over empty tables
as if glancing up at frescoes
in the picture gallery, or guarding the unused gate
of a home for the incurably romantic.

Today, returning from a walk beyond the town walls,
we have taken the wrong road,
toward the psychiatric hospital, and doubling back
I become strangely indecisive,
noticing from the bridge Via dei Malcontenti
figures on the bell tower
taking in the view (the cypresses beyond us
like some painted backdrop) – snippets of people
moving crablike at the barbizonned edge.
So that when I see, below, a woman hang out her wash
I feel my being wrung from me
as though it might defy evaporation
while she scans with nonchalance
this bridge so far from our goal,
another bridge we need not have crossed.

5: In Florence, at the Pension Pitti Palace, Its Final Season

There are days I fear
I've done nothing in life,

consuming water, earth, and air
others might have better mixed

to create something worth the while
of this time before the fires.

There are days I've been critical
of those I knew meant well.

I think of the monks and nuns
who gave such faithful service

to a world dismissing them
as antedeluvian.

I don't want to become a bore:
I feel I care too much.

I have lost my good humour
yet often against my will

I've been understanding
to the point of condescension.

I have distanced those who loved me,
I've been too kind to strangers.

I need the courage to be prickly,
more light, much more life.

6: At Santa Maria del Fiore, Its Dome Raised Without Scaffolding

Every night I dream about you;
I forget what you're trying to say.

I'm becoming wary of dreams;
recurring ones especially

mean unfinished business.
In the dining car of a train

I ate alone beside a window,
when I saw a woman on a horse

fail to keep pace with us.
She smiled and waved – at me.

In her life there was a crossing
to reach before the train,

and in her wave a gift
with no thanks expected.

How can any of us leave
knowing with certainty

whether we will be missed?
I need to return changed.

I saw a horse I wanted to ride.
I saw a woman on my way south

who in trying to race a train
remembered to smile.

7: At the Galleria dell'Accademica

David so filled a modern artist with dread,
he smashed one marble toe,
and we who wonder as supplicants, visitors,
are awed not only by the forgiving stone
but by the deliberate disproportion,

the head, arms, legs Michelangelo
magnified in this slayer of giants,
leaving the buttocks and much of the rest
perfect as no man should be,
even one with a Biblical stare.

What, given such conscious desecration,
can it mean to restore fragments,
and whose lifetime are they returned to?
Perhaps this cross, or inlaid crozier,
or chalice should be transmuted

to something no one could appraise
until his own Day of Judgement.
Yet there are injuries we all bear
beyond our natural rates of decline,
which is why we come to such places:

as if studied imperfections
were artistically acceptable flaws
in beauties that still have power
to entrance us, no less than dismay us.
No one who breathes the air survives.

Tourist Quota

The Road to Kandahar

We are not on the road to Kandahar. It is in Afghanistan, which I confused as a boy with the North-West Frontier Province. There is also a Kandahar in Saskatchewan, a western Canadian province, on a highway called the Yellowhead. It was named for a blond Indian.

There is also a Ceylon. The railway named it Ceylon because the local postmaster did not want it named after him. His name was Aldred.

We are on a highway of sorts from Hassan to Sravanabelagola, also called Shravan Belgola, often simply S. Belgola. This highway has no name, but I suspect people from S. Belgola call it Hassan Road while people from Hassan call it S. Belgola Road.

We are going to see the statue of Lord Bahubali, also called Gomateshvara, also "the monk on the top of the hill". According to our guidebook, the statue is seventeen metres high, over fifty feet. It is the largest monolithic statue in the world, a modern Colossus of Rhodes, but I am more taken by the road. I would like to think there is no poetry in the names of places we glimpse. I am looking for stories, after all.

Boovanahally
Kenchatahally
Heggadehally
Vaddarakoppalu
Ranganathapura

Hally means small village – in Kannada, my father's mother tongue. He grew up speaking Kannada. He settled in Canada.

Byadarehally
Muddanahalli
Appenahali
Dandiganahalli
Madenur

These places do not appear on maps of India. They do not even appear on maps of Karnataka. This is the proper name of my home state, but I often call it Mysore. It was renamed after state boundaries were redrawn on linguistic lines. That happened the year I was born, so I can call it Mysore if I wish.

On the map of Saskatchewan linger places that barely exist. Settlements like Carpenter, named for one H.S. Carpenter, a deputy minister of highways. He, in turn, was named for the Henry Stanley who rediscovered Doctor Livingstone. Nothing exists of Carpenter except a few houses and perhaps a sign. Now H.S. is better remembered for his grandson, David Carpenter, author of books with intriguing titles like *Jokes for the Apocalypse*.

Choudenhalli
Upinahally
Baraguru
Katharighatta
Channarayapatna, also called C.R. Patna
Hosur

In our stairway hang two paintings of Archive, Saskatchewan. Good name, Archive, since it also barely exists except in memories of maps, on maps of memory. Sometimes the railway named towns in alphabetic order, so Archive precedes Buttress, Crestwynd, Dunkirk and Expanse. One will even find names beginning with unlikely letters. Q is for Quantock. Z is for Zumbro.

Kandahar was not named Kandahar because it followed a town with a name beginning with J. The railway named it for a famous battle during the Afghan War, a battle the British won. A town named for a British victory and settled by Norwegians.

Nor was Cochin named Cochin because it followed a town with a name beginning with B. Nor was it named for the Cochin in Kerala, on the west coast of India: the Cochin famed for Chinese fishing nets, even a synagogue. The Co-*shun* in Saskatchewan is not even pronounced like the Co-*chin* in Kerala. Cochin, Saskatchewan, was named for Reverend Father Louis Cochin, who lived on reserves called Poundmaker and Thunderchild.

It is now after noon. We have ascended the six hundred fourteen steps of Indragiri Hill, towering south of S. Belgola. We have seen Lord Bahubali, and we have descended. We have ascended the three hundred odd steps of neighbouring Chandragiri Hill. We have seen Jain temples, called *bastis*, and we have descended.

On the way back to Hassan, I am once more taken by the road, by names of places we glimpse. I am weary of making connections. I would like to think I am weary of finding poetry where none should exist. But I am not, and it does.

Ghandarayapatna, not called G.R. Patna
Malenhalli
A.G. Hally
Yeliyur
Udiyapur

Annenahally
Hirahalli
Karekere
H. Aladahally

Shantigrama
Tyavalli
Samudrahalli
Chickenegere

Such places do not appear on maps of India or even of Karnataka, which I often call Mysore. On the map of Saskatchewan linger places that barely exist.

Mumbai, Jumbai

Bombay (now officially Mumbai) has had lots of official name changes which everyone completely ignores. – *India: A Travel Survival Kit*

Good morning, ladies. Good morning, gents. I am honoured to welcome you to this luxury tour of India's gateway, known to you as Bombay. I am not the usual tour guide. I am not even a guide by intent. I was meant to be an historian. Alas, Mother India has little use in these times for a Ph.D. (Failed). Think of me as your guide *pro tempore.*

We are standing now on Nariman Point, the Manhattan of India. The very land on which we stand has been reclaimed. If you look northwest across Back Bay, you will perceive the far end of the Queen's Necklace. It curves through two hundred and twenty-five degrees of the compass – from Malabar Point in the west, past Malabar Hill to Chowpatty Beach in the north, then southeast along Marine Drive to this very spot. The necklace remains largely invisible throughout the haze of day. At dusk it appears with the stars: neon rubies, helium sapphires, krypton emeralds, and (twinkling among these unlikely, earthly gems) a sprinkling of diamonds from the tungsten of household lamps.

Directly south of us you will note a smaller bay, a bite of bay on whose far shore is Cuffe Parade and, beyond that, Colaba Point. This is the most expensive real estate in India.

Not there, sir. Not there, madam. I am speaking of this land at our feet that is still under water. Engineers are reclaiming it from the sea. What, you may wonder, does one call someone who brokers land that is still under water? An unreal-estate agent? Buying and selling are the blood of Bombay. So is reclaiming land in our blood, and much of what you know as Bombay is land reclaimed.

Those who are not preoccupied with reclaiming land are preoccupied with renaming it. This is because Mother India is still attempting to recover her history from the predations of British rule. Thus, visitors to Bombay should note that Bombay is no longer called Bombay. It is called Mumbai. This is the city's official name, just as Varanasi, known under the Raj as Benares, is once again called Varanasi.

And what, you may wonder, is the origin of Bombay's new name?

Mumbai is not a new name. It is an old name – so old, its earliest usage is lost to us in antiquarian mists. We know that Ptolemy, the Greek geographer of the second century, called this place Heptanesia for the seven islands that once were here, namely, Colaba, Mahim, Parel, Worli, Girgaum, Dongri and Mazgaon. Heptanesia faded from the historical records of your Occidental antecedents till the Hindu king Bhimdev occupied it in the thirteenth century. Then came the Sultans of Gujarat. Then, in the sixteenth century, came the Portuguese. All this time, the islands were inhabited by simple fisherfolk known as the Kolis. Who but folk of the utmost simplicity could eke a living among tidal swamps and mudflats fit only for mosquitoes?

When the Portuguese arrived, they found the largest of these islands to be called Mumbai. This was after a deity of the Kolis, Mumba Aai. It may be difficult to find a descendant of such simple fisherfolk these days. It is not so difficult to find Mumba's temple, which has been rebuilt and relocated. You may find it off Kalbadevi Road.

No, sir. No, madam. We shall not be going there.

In 1534 the Sultan of Gujarat ceded all seven islands to the Portuguese. They renamed Mumbai as Bom Bahai, Good Bay. It afforded shelter for seagoing craft, but soon the Portuguese found the swamps and mudflats no fit place for a trading post. They looked for someone on whom to offload this place, and who better on whom to offload a colony than the acquisitive British? This was in 1662, when Catherine of Braganza married King Charles II, that Merry Monarch of the Restoration. The British renamed Bom Bahai as Bom Baim, still the Good Bay. Precisely two centuries later, in 1862, all seven islands were joined as one. This is what you claim to know as Bombay but which every right-thinking son and daughter of Mother India ought to call Mumbai.

And now, not only has the city been renamed but so also have its thoroughfares. Gone are the old British names. Kindly erase them from your consciousness. In their stead are Indian names and even some Portuguese ones.

Yes, sir. Yes, madam. I predicted you would ask as much. Why should this be so, given that, along with Christianity, the Portuguese brought the Inquisition to India? I can only assume it is because they arrived before the British and so belong to a more distant, less painful (and, perhaps, more romantic) past.

Are there other questions? God be praised.

To continue with an example, the portion of the Queen's Necklace known as Marine Drive has been renamed. It is now Netaji Subash Road. Mind you, it is one thing to rename a city. Renaming streets is a different matter, for many of us who grew up here did so using the British names. As a result, some of you may find that in order to locate Netaji Subash Road you will have to ask for Marine Drive.

This is a small price to pay for reclaiming history. The confusion is, like my own status in life, a temporary one and does not hint (not one iota) at failure. Allow me then, while we still await stragglers, to introduce you to Mumbai from A to Z, the new streetname first, the old name subsequent.

No, sir. No, madam. It is correctly pronounced *zed*. Even the most Disneyfied among us do not say *zee*.

Apollo Pier Road is now known as Shivaji Maharaj Marg. This is after Shivaji, that hero of old Maharashtra who not only challenged the Mughals of Delhi but also, having been born a mere artisan or serf, proved that one need not be a Brahmin to succeed in this temporal world of ours. Now, if you will kindly repeat after me:

Amrit Keshav Nayak Marg — not Bastion Road
Mahadeo Palao Marg — not Curry Road
Kale Marg — not De-provincialised Road

That is precisely what I said: De-provincialised Road.

J. Bhatankar Marg — not Elphinstone Road
R.S. Marg — not Gunbow Street
Dr. E. Borges Avenue — not Hospital Avenue

No, sir. No, madam. I do not know whether this Dr. Borges is any relation to the Argentine writer Jorge Luis Borges but, yes, I do relish that writer's juxtaposition of fiction, reality, and philosophical reflection. After me, if you please:

Barfiwala Lane — not Juhu Lane
Dr. Annie Besant Road — not Love Grove, certainly not
Dr. Mascarenhas Road — not Mount Road

Mascarenhas is a good Portuguese name. I am not familiar with this particular doctor but an explorer of the sixteenth century, one Pedro de Mascarenhas, gave his name to the Mascarene Islands of the Indian Ocean, namely, Mauritius, Rodriguez, and Réunion. Repeat, please:

Laxmibai Jagmohandas Marg — not Nepean Sea Road
Shahid Bhagat Singh Road — not Old Custom House Road
Bhagoji Keer Marg — not Paradise Cinema Lane

R.B. Mehta Road — not Sixty Feet Road
Senapati Bapat Marg — not Tulsi Pipe Road
Nathalal Parekh Marg — not Wodehouse Road

No, sir. No, madam. I do not know whether this was the same P.G. Wodehouse who created the fictitious gentleman Bertie Wooster and his gentleman's gentleman, Jeeves.

Last, we have Y Road, now known as Bal Govindas Road. Are there any further questions? God be praised.

In conclusion, I should warn you that a number of landmarks have also been renamed. Victoria Garden is now Jijamata Udyan. Do not assume, however, that there is no use hunting out the famous Flora Fountain by its old name. This was the monument erected to honour Sir Henry Bartle Edward Frere. He was governor when Bombay became a cotton-polis in the 1860s thanks to the cotton shortages caused by your American Civil War – the very man responsible for joining the seven islands of Bombay into one. The place christened Flora Fountain has been renamed Hutatma Chowk, or Martyrs' Square. The reasons for this must await my noon-hour discourse on the importance of Maharastra State to the Indian Union.

Do not assume there is no use hunting out Flora Fountain, I say, for in order to discover Hutatma Chowk you may still have to ask for the Fountain. As for the Hanging Gardens, they are more correctly, though not always, known as Pherozeshah Mehta Gardens. By the by, these gardens are stepped across three tanks that supply water to the city. They are not hanged.

There you have it, ladies. Your humble servant, gents. Mumbai from A to Z. Even as the engineers of Bombay are reclaiming land, we who cherish our past are also reclaiming it. Not by dredging soil and dumping stone. Not by rolling back the sea. We are doing so by rolling back history itself. Which of these is the more difficult? Who can say? And what if these attempts amount to the same thing: rolling back history, rolling back the sea? I often wonder about the English King Canute, he who wished to teach his councillors the limits of even a king's power. Would he have felt as powerless had he hailed from Bombay? From, well, that is to say –

Yes, sir. Yes, madam. You may now board the bus.

How Very Practical the Indian

(After Selwyn Gurney Champion's *Racial Proverbs: A Selection of the World's Proverbs Arranged Linguistically*.)

Readers who look for anything very philosophical in Indian proverbs will be disappointed. You will find how very practical the Indian is. India is a land of villages to be judged by its own standards. Thus you must look at the country of the one-eyed with one eye. Here then are some proverbs of the Indian, whose wit is often bucolic:

Agriculture is the best profession;
trade is middling good;
service barely rates a mention;
as a last resort, beg.

Some things can only be got after the owner dies:
the hair of a tiger, the tusk of an elephant,
the breast of a chaste woman, the sword of a brave man,
the gem of a snake, and the riches of a Brahmin.
These three always quarrel among themselves:
Brahmins, dogs, and poets.
If we see a dog there is no stone;
if we see a stone there is no dog.

It is a brave bird that makes its nest in a cat's ear.
A cat is a lion in a jungle of small bushes.
Where there are no trees, the castor-oil plant is chief.
Among the noseless, the man with nostrils is "Mr. Nose".
The mother-in-law is great, the daughter-in-law is great;
the pot is burning; who will take it off the fire?
A potter's donkey will follow anyone with muddy trousers.
There is a thick mist, so sing as you please.

These are the signs of a rogue:
a face like the petals of a lotus, excessive humility,
a heart like a pair of scissors, and a voice as cool as scandal.

The world is a theatre of love.
I went in search of love and lost myself.
For sweetness, honey; for love, a wife.
If the bullock and the cart keep together,
what does it matter how many ups and downs there are?
A woman's word is a bundle of water.
A woman's thoughts are afterthoughts.
Educating a woman is like giving a monkey a knife.
Money left in the hands of a woman won't last;
a child left in the hands of a man won't live.
A man thinks he knows, but a woman knows better.
If you love your love, love her thoughts as well.

There is no hand to catch time.
When you see a cloud speckled like the wing of a partridge
and a widow applying scented oil to her hair,
one will rain; the other will elope.
A motherless child is like a curry without onions.
The dead child of a married woman has only gone out to play.
Death is the black camel that kneels before every door.
If you worry, this will bring you to the grave,
but if you do not worry you will never die.
Man comes into the world with his hands shut
and goes out of it with his hands open.
Are the lines of the hand ever rubbed out?

Love knows no lowly caste;
hunger minds not stale repast;
thirst knows not the ghat whereon the dead are burned;
no broken cot has sleep been known to spurn.

Write a nibful more; eat a mouthful less.
Honour and profit are not found in the same dish.
The stomach has no ear; the hungry cannot hear.
The poor seek food; the rich seek an appetite.
To feet that wear sandals the whole world is leather.

The rich man will feed the rich man;
the poor man will feed the rich man.
A fat man has no religion.

Do not be miserable for the sake of pleasure.
Eat coconuts while you have your teeth.
Call on God, but row away from the rocks.
Beware the guru who is a glutton.
Beware the door with several keys.
Why seek the key of an open door?
If you believe, it is a deity; otherwise it is a stone.
When the eyes are closed, the world is dark.
Write like the learned; speak like the masses.
Anger has no eyes.

You cannot take one part of a fowl for cooking
and leave the other part to lay eggs.
If you stir the rubbish heap of a barber,
you will turn up only hair.
Nothing to bother you, eh? Then go buy a goat.

Do not believe a weeping man or a laughing woman.
Fear the well-fed clown and the hungry gentleman.
Distrust the man who hates the taste of curds,
the scent of clover, and the song of birds.
Live far from relatives and near water.
Wear torn things but be independent.
Do not adjust your hat under a pear tree,
nor tie your shoes in a melon patch.
Be the eleventh person among ten.

Wisdom has not vanished; the wise have vanished.
Good travels at a snail's pace but evil has wings.
No one was ever lost on a straight road.
Mat-makers do not lie on mats.

A bear is an unsafe bedfellow.
Evening is the mother of patience.
Every European who comes to India acquires
patience if he has none, and loses it if he has.
Never speak to a white man till after he has eaten.
Oh, and did you hear? A demon took a monkey to wife;
the result, by the grace of God, was the English.

Tampering

Begamudre means Lockseal. The first of our clan works in a royal treasury. Each night he locks it, sews a cloth around the lock, stamps the royal seal onto wax. Next morning, if he finds the seals cracked, he will know that someone has broken in.

My grandfather begins life as Begamudre Nelawanki Krishna-Rao, Nelawanki the name of his father's village. After his father loses his land, my grandfather becomes B. Krishna-Rao, a man with no land to his name.

He names my father Rakosh, formally B. Rakosh-Das, after a Freemason named Rakoczi. His mother calls him Rakoshi or, when impatient, Rakosh-Das. She names her favourite son Ananda. It means happiness or joy.

When my mother is pregnant (with me) she prays to Lord Venkateswara for a son, promises to name him after the Lord. I am born B. Venkateswara, sometimes Venkatesh.

Ashbury College, Ottawa, day one. Mrs. Dalton is taking roll. When she asks for my family name, I give it. When she asks for my given name, I give that, too. She takes both my names and gives me back Venkatesh Begamudre. At once I have been reborn and christened.

We use only last names at Ashbury. Brothers pose no problem. We have a Luciano One and a Luciano Two. Classmates find Begamudre too long. To them I become V.B. Who am I to deny them the comfort of abbreviations? This is their land.

My mother's parents name her Lakshmi, formally Lakshmi-Bai, after the goddess of wealth. My father calls her Lakshmi-Bai. She calls him sir.

He cringes when she calls me Babu, Boy in her mother tongue. He thinks Babu too soft. He thinks me too soft. He calls me either V.B. or Boy. His hand, when it strikes, is not soft.

Since my father and I have different last names, people ask if I am adopted. Sometimes I wonder, too. He will later reverse his name to match mine. By then it will no longer matter (to me) whose son I am.

Mrs. Going ("Call me Granny.") is my first baby sitter. She thinks my given name, now also my first, is Venkatish. Shortens it to Tish. That's what people later call me in Kingston. That and, "Tissue, I need you, achoo!"

"Reach for the Top", Vancouver, first night of taping. A technician finds Venkatesh too long for the acrylic sign he fabricates. He shortens it to Ven. Thank you, Lord.

Some people hear it as Ben. Others ask, "As in Venn diagram?" Friends reply, "As in vending machine," and I pretend amusement. Two men, scholars and gentlemen, say *min vän* means my friend in Swedish. I consider moving.

Schiller College, Paris, day one. The principal keeps dropping the last *e* in Begamudre. When I say it's pronounced like an *a*, she adds an *accent aigu*. People appear bemused especially since, thanks to a professor named J.J. Van Vlasselaer, I speak French with a Belgian accent.

Back in India now, my cousins try hard to call me Ven. I wish they wouldn't. I wish I were the same Venkatesh who left as a boy. Someone has been in the treasury. We know because the seals are cracked. The lock has not been forced, but even a cursory inspection reveals tampering.

Technicolor

I am discovering speech under Mascarene skies. My father lives in America and plans to raise me there, so he asks my grandmother to teach me English instead of their mother tongue. This is why, when I later live with my mother, while we wait to rejoin him, she takes me to only American movies. Dumbo learns to fly. The Swiss Family Robinson races ostriches, battles pirates. The Sleeping Beauty sleeps under blue American skies. But I want to see an Indian movie, a film. What happens in an Indian film?

Swearing me to secrecy, my grandmother takes me. It's in her mother tongue. It's in black and white. In an early scene, Lord Krishna reclines on a window ledge and plays his flute. Villainous guards swing their swords at him, perhaps through him, in vain. In the final scene warriors on horseback assemble in a courtyard while the evil king, mortally wounded, crawls to his death. The warriors cheer their new king and fireworks burst over the palace. White fireworks, in a black and white sky.

Fairy Tales

My mother told me, *Planes don't crash.*

Nineteen fifty-nine. There are no direct flights from the Mascarene Islands, east of Madagascar, to India. We fly northwest to Nairobi, northeast to Bombay. I am three. The plane drops in storms, then climbs, propellers chewing air. *Don't be worried,* she says. *If we go too low, we simply bounce back up. There is a spring under the tail.*

In Canada now, I can't find my favourite toy, a battery operated elephant. A ping pong ball would bounce, as if on a spring, in air hissing from the upraised trunk. *Oh,* she says. *I sent it by sea mail. The Chinese sank the ship.* That night I dream a battle at sea. Turbaned men with scimitars fight, hand to hand, on battleship grey decks.

At eight, my tonsils must go. *Don't be worried,* she says. *Boys who have their tonsils removed grow tall.*

Tafelmusik Performs the "Other" Brandenburg Concertos

That white winter I turned thirteen, I saw my first
string quartet. The Vaghy Quartet. Four men so brave
they faced down five hundred pairs of pupils
more used to skits on that stage than strings. Don't ask me
what they played. All I would ever remember
was the cellist. He was black. A lot of my heroes were black
back then – Sidney Poitier, Arthur Ashe – but an Indian kid
had to find heroes where he could. And better than serving ace
after ace, Ashe wore glasses. Now Poitier tries to act wise
in the shadows of less gentle men. Ashe is dead.
My heroes have names like Kingsley, Te Kanawa.
Jon Kimura Parker – a Japanese Canadian I met calls him a Halfer.

Turning thirty-seven today, I find myself far from home
as usual, in a church of all things,
while a bearded giant in a cummerbund plays an oboe,
bent over it as if over a straw. Washington McClain:
good name for a man who might've been a linebacker once.
I love it when he lifts his eyes from the music. Not to me;
to the first violin, those belled cheeks asking, *Allegro?*
Molto? Later, taking his bows with the rest, he seems
unaware of the stir his trousers cause, the dye more indigo
than black. Outside, blizzards pound the seaboard
from Labrador to Alabama. The power is out in Tennessee.

Back in our mixed neighbourhood, as in white collar and blue,
Robert Holmes the ex-Roughrider renovates his house.
He grins. I grin. He says, *Howza goin'*. I say, *Howza goin'*.
Other times, near the corner store, I see other
black men. They can tell I'm not one of them.
And though they ignore the whites hurrying past the cathedral,
they often stop and say hello. Sometimes we shake hands.
Brothers passing in the street? I don't think so.
But they take me back to the summer I looked up from a book

and what should I see but a black man
carrying his cello down our lane? It was late afternoon
and it was perfect: that a man should carry a cello home
at quitting time; that such men live and work and play among us,
and always have. So tell me something, J.B.:

When you were trying to score that job
from the Margrave of Brandenburg,
did you ever guess how many savage breasts
your music would one day soothe?

Playing for Time

For the tenth fall in as many years, you're putting the garden
to bed. Harvesting tomatoes: fried green for breakfast, red and
raw for lunch. The neighbours' girl, the one we call our niece,
likes the little ones best. Wednesday it snowed. Overnight, the
creeper dulled, and the robins have stopped on their way south.
Even the clowns

are back, grey-green birds we still don't know what to call. Me,
I'm at the piano staving off middle age. My way of checking for
a pulse. Friends understand, like they understood the model
trains: N-scale, HO. Why I put them away. Why the lessons
once a week. More scales: similar motion, contrary motion,
triads. This time last year it was

"Greensleeves". Now it's Bach, "Prelude" to *The Well-Tempered
Clavier*. Two notes on the left hand, sixteenths on the right,
two eighth-note rests. No wonder I get lost. All those flowing,
broken chords – *piano, fortissimo*, up, down, sideways. Then that
crescendo poco a poco, except I start too soft or end too loud. Then
that bloody arpeggio. Sure, it's nice

outside, but in here there's laundry and dishes and dustballs.
I would've been a house slave way down south, more at home
with keys than compost. And though the notes are slurred,
Gould played them crisp. He liked his Bach crisp. Like all the
leaves you crackle searching for one last red in this frostbitten
grey-green. When I offer to help

you call: *Only if you want.* You know I don't. I loved this garden
once. Then we took out the sod. Dug up the play area no one
plays in, not even our niece. There's no one here her age. Nearly
was, though. Come Christmas, we'll give her the Timberwolf
and Redwood, G-scale, its engine a foot long. Someone has to
put the garden to bed. Every child should have a train.

Postcolonial Eulogies for the Grandfather I Never Met

1. From the *Bulletin of the Calcutta Mathematical Society*, volume 40, 1948 (page 49):

Membership: The Council learns with a deep sorrow of the death of Professor C.V. Hanumanta Rao, whose services as a former Vice-president and a member of the Board of Editors of the *Bulletin* the Council recalls with grateful appreciation.

During the year under review four new members were elected.

2. From an article, "The Dual of a Theorem Proved by F. Morely", published by Henry Frederick Baker, Cambridge University, in a later number of volume 40, 1948 (page 226):

I learn with deep regret, from the March number of the *Bulletin of the Calcutta Mathematical Society*, that my old and much respected friend, C.V. Hanumanta Rao, formerly Professor at Lahore, has died. So far as I know his last publications related to a theorem variously known by the names of Petersen, Hjelmslev and Morely, taken in projective form. I should like to offer the following lines for publication in tribute to my late friend. They were actually written in correspondence with him about his last two papers; and, as will be seen, the result might appropriately be named for him.

In ordinary space of three dimensions, let u, v, w, u′ ,v′, w′ be six lines, passing through a point T, which lie on a quadric cone. If we take any two ordered triads from these lines, say u, v, w and u′, v′, w′, and consider the six planes α=(v′,w), α'=(v,w′), β=(w′,u), β'=(w,u′), γ=(u′,v), γ'=(u,v′), then the three lines of intersection of pairs of these, (α,α'), (β,β'), (γ,γ'), lie in a plane through T. . . .

3. From an interview with my Aunt Rama Menon in Vancouver, July 21, 1995, shortly before her 65th birthday:

Dates and places, I am not sure. It says in my diary – here it is – Daddy was born 29th October, 1892. Does not say when he died.

Nineteen forty-seven, yes. It must have been after 15th August, because we were independent.

No, Mommy's father was a civil engineer. Daddy's father was a schools' inspector. You might ask Papalu, he knows dates and places. He is like you, always asking what happened when.

Daddy caught tuberculosis in Lahore during the riots, the Hindu-Muslim riots. He had grown a beard so people would think he was Muslim and he would be safe. Then, one day, he was sitting reading the newspaper in his hotel, and a Hindu fellow tried to cut him with a knife! Daddy was a strong man. He survived.

Fifty-five when he died, correct.

No, the doctor did not tell him it was TB. Mommy hid it from us but I suspected. He lost so much weight. I took care of him. I checked his temperature morning and evening, but he did not want us spending time and effort keeping him alive. Would not allow them to collapse his lungs. He encouraged me to apply for medical school. I did not get in. It is all right. I would take care of birds that fell from our *neem* tree. Poor things, they were so frightened. It is all right I did not get in.

Temple Bay

On the beach at Mahabalipuram, sand crabs play jute with the sea. *It's a game we played as children,* I say. *If the one who was It came too close, you could squat with a hand on your head and yell, "Jute!" and you couldn't be tagged.* So it is now while the sun sets: the world cannot touch us.

Last night, returning from the Shore Temple after photographing its towers, we prayed the long dark streaks taunting us meant no harm. Now we see it's true: dun crabs peering from holes run toward waves cresting pink, then back, swerving to evade water. Laugh: we laugh until one, the largest yet, heads right out to sea and vanishes. Others follow. We decide they know what they're doing.

In the morning this sea – in fact a bay, the Bay of Bengal – is green. Pale green where waves curl back onto themselves. Afternoons, it's blue. Now it's electric blue, electric green; olive drab where it churns the sand. Coppery. If we place our feet just so, the sand changes colour in halos like all the footprints of gods you photograph. Imagine: the weight of our passing leaves auras.

You: *Look at those clouds!* Massing above the sea, their centres white, a misty pink at the edge – translucent clouds veiling a blue streak. Now butterflies appear from the sun. They skim the dunes and also head out to sea. They'll come back. They're safe in places like this, where elements meet. Sun. Sea. Sand. Sky. At times like these. Twilight. Dawn.

At Kanyakumari, you say, *where this bay meets an ocean and a sea, on the evening of the full moon you can watch sunset and moonrise together. Both at once?* I ask; then, *We'll go there, yes, one day.* For now, I can't imagine being anywhere but here.

Oh! you say. *Look.* From where we stand, the temple towers have overlapped. One triangle where before there were two. Fishermen claim the gods Vishnu and Shiva lived here. Durga, as well. Three gods in one temple. But there's more: the fishermen say that once there stood seven temples. The sea claimed the other six – intact, still, underwater. Fishermen know these things.

Tonight the moon will be almost full, more dazzling than we've seen it back home. That man in the moon will look less surprised, more knowing somehow. Tonight Venus will rise above her own reflection. But that's not all. She will glide ashore. If she places her feet in the auras of our passing, it will mean we are still in love.

Unaccompanied Cello Suites

You, by the window, read of art history from ancient Harappa's lord of the beasts to the Taj Mahal. Pause to watch the present pass: hedgeplants, sugar cane. Rest your eyes on type, the safety of numbered pages. And here we are jolting inland to the holiest hill in the South. Yes, getting there is half the fun but India's too much in me to read. Or sightsee. I take refuge in your Walkman while speakers blare Bhangra pop, Tamil pop. *Han han aam aam yeah yeah*. Indians are not only stone deaf, they're tone deaf.

Slowing. Unscheduled. You, pulling me: *Look at this!* You see a man crouched like a monkey. Not just any monkey: Hanuman himself. Complete with golden mace, golden skin, monkey jaws blending oh so prosthetically into a red monkey face. *Can you not give money, ladies? Even a little, gents?* Bloody guide. Wouldn't answer questions about my family god. All aflutter now, all agog. *He is debasing himself, poor fellow, to raise necessary funds. To raise Hanuman temple for his village.*

You, coaxing: *Let's give a bit.* Meaning, if I can't spare rupees I can part with a smile. Rupees then. A five you try handing the guide grasping spontaneous offers. Mainly twos. Too late, he's out, he's back. Hanuman waves his thanks. And when a pale green note flutters from your window, he bows over clasped hands. You, ecstatic: *He was perfect. You should've seen him!* But I did, I insist, though not really: a flash of paint, a monkey face, a flick of ropey tail. I leave you with reflections of an India I can't face, even glassed in. You leave me to Yo-Yo Ma. The melody and broken chords of a *Sarabande*.

We, on Commercial Street, spend our last night in my home town buying mirror work, *churidar* sets, Narayan's *The Emerald Route* – in Cantonment, the British preserve where after the Raj my mother bought me clothes at Kiddie's Corner. We're spending rupees we can't take with us. Split up to splurge efficiently. You, alone, encounter an Indian Santa ringing his cowbell. An honest-to-God Santa Claus I miss for keeping one eye out for our hired car inching through crowds. Not Christmas shoppers. Commercial Street's always busy after dark. *Grotesque,* you say. *A gunny-sack belly, a rat's-nest beard, sweat streaking his greasepaint face, brown showing through made-up white skin.* You, appalled: *He was so grotesque. Too bad you missed him.*

Now that, yes, I wish I had seen. All the same, it's not true I don't see things. I simply don't share so much till later, when of course I share too much. Although once, on our veranda while you slept in that posh cabin at Mahabalipuram, you'll never believe what I saw. The Shore Temple grew distinct under a rising moon – hardly unusual, till the sea people started coming ashore. They were dark. They left their boats to wade through shoals with lions, tigers, cheetahs. Surged back for elephants while those lumbering cats paced in the surf. Dark. They were dark even thirteen hundred years ago.

I came this close to waking you.

Acknowledgements

Since I spent about ten years, from 1989 to 1999, writing the pieces in this book and another six years revising them, the earlier drafts of most of these pieces have been published or broadcast in Canada, Scotland and Australia.

The long poem "The Lightness Which is Our World, Seen from Afar" is my tropical response to Patrick Lane's *Winter* (Coteau Books). Three excerpts appeared in *Because You Loved Being a Stranger* (Harbour Publishing); the entire poem appeared in *Chapman* and *The Capilano Review*.

"Itineraries" contains my translations, from English to English, of poems in Jay Meek's *Stations* (Carnegie Mellon University Press). "Itineraries" appeared in *Grain*.

Various pieces in "Tourist Quota" appeared in the periodicals *Border Crossings*, *Canadian Literature*, *Geist*, *Mattoid*, *Passages*, *Prairie Fire* and *TickleAce*; in the textbook *Insights: Immigrant Experiences* (Harcourt Brace Canada); in the chapbook *The Neighbouring Heart* (Cathedral Village Arts Festival); and on "Gallery", produced by CBC Radio in Saskatchewan. Some pieces have been recorded for radio by The Banff Centre for the Arts and filmed for television by Incandescent Films.

The epigraph to "Mumbai, Jumbai" is from page 523 of *India: A Travel Survival Kit* (Lonely Planet Publications, 3rd ed., 1987). "How Very Practical the Indian" is based on pages 393 to 438 of Selwyn Gurney Champion's *Racial Proverbs: A Selection of the World's Proverbs Arranged Linguistically* (Routledge & Kegan Paul Ltd., 2nd ed., 1950) and on pages lx to lxi, "Introduction to the Proverbs of India" by H.N. Randle.

If I listed everyone who influenced this book (and I'm sure they know who they are), there would be little room for the work itself; but two people deserve special mention. I'm fairly sure that Anne Szumigalski (1922-1999) felt that knowing how to live is just as important as knowing how to write. I'm also fairly sure that my ex-wife, Shelley Sopher, would agree.

Photo by Lynne Beclu

Ven Begamudré was born in South India and moved to Canada when he was six. He has also lived in Mauritius and the United States. These days, he divides his time between western Canada and the island of Bali.